Sheheen, Dennis(illus)

A child's picture dictionary,
English/Chinese

	DATE DUE	

Library of Congress Cataloging-in-Publication Data

Sheheen, Dennis, 1944-
  A child's picture dictionary, English/Chinese.

  Summary: A Chinese/English picture dictionary with an illustrated selection of words accompanying each letter of the alphabet. Illustrations are identified in both languages.
  1. Picture dictionaries, Chinese. 2. Picture dictionaries, English. 3. Chinese language — Dictionaries, Juvenile. 4. English language — Dictionaries, Juvenile.
[1. Picture dictionaries, Chinese. 2. Picture dictionaries. 3. Chinese language materials — Bilingual]
I. Title.
PL1423.S53   1987   495.1'321   87-17399
ISBN 1-55774-001-1

Printed in Israel
Adama Books, 306 West 38 Street, New York, New York 10018

A Child's Picture Dictionary

English/Chinese

illustrated by Dennis Sheheen

Adama Books   New York

Aa

automobile
di shē
的 士

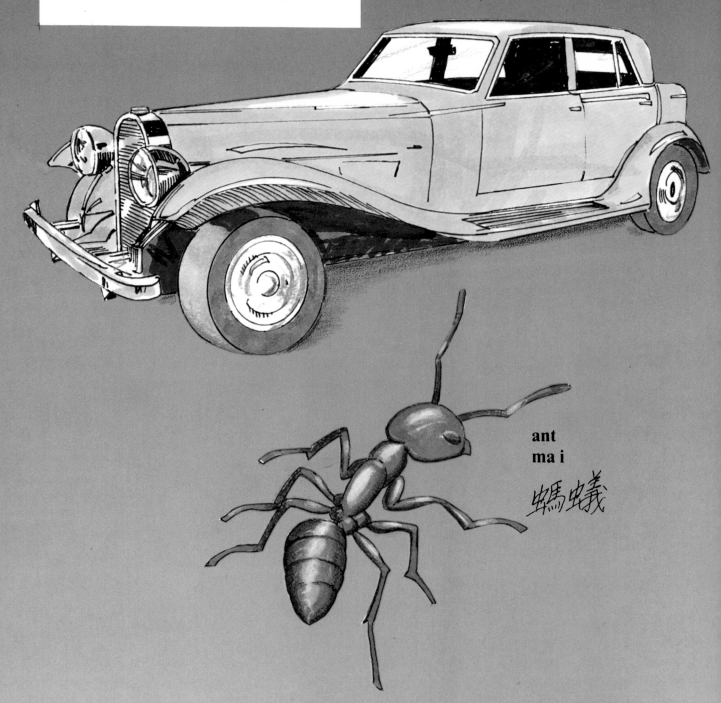

ant
ma i
螞蟻

airplane
fay chē

飛機

apple
pin gaw

萍菓

Bb

butterfly
hū dĭp
蝴蝶

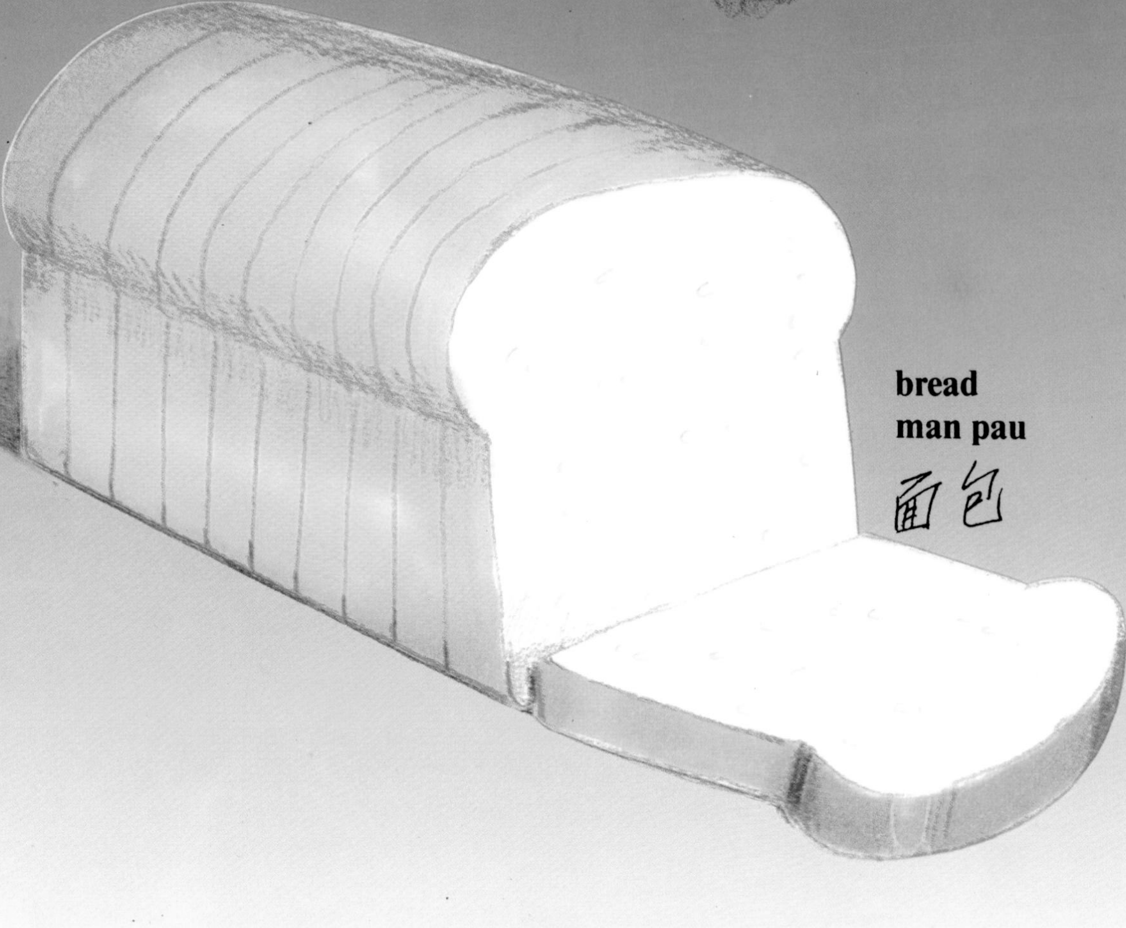

bread
man pau
面包

banana
hū ǒwm zēū

香蕉

ball
pǎ

波

Cc

camel
loto
馬各馬它

clown
stē-ō chou
小丑

cloud
one
雲

cat
mǎo
猫

coat
low
褸

Dd

dog
gow
狗

drink
yum
飲

doorknob
men pa sow

門把手

doll
kung tsi

公仔

door
men

門

Ee

FOR YOU

envelope
hsin feng
信封

egg
guy tan
雞蛋

eye
yen
眼

elephant
ta pen cheng

大笨象

Ff

frog
tien chi

田雞

foot
gǐo

脚

finger
shou chi
手指

fish
yu
魚

flower
fa
花

Gg

giraffe
chang ching lu
長頸鹿

gift
li mi
禮物

glass
pa le buoy
玻璃杯

giant
gō-ē yen
巨人

Hh

hamburger
han bow bao
漢堡飽

house
wu
屋

Ii

igloo
ping wu
冰屋

iron
tang tou
尉火斗

island
doe
島

Jj

jacket
fei gay shu
飛機恤

juggler
pien hey fa
變戲法

jigsaw puzzle
chi how pan
七巧板

Kk

key
saw see
鎖匙

kite
chi yao
紙鳶

kangaroo
tai shu
袋鼠

L1

lips
tsui shun
嘴唇

leg
tui
腿

lion
see ze
獅子

Mm

mother
ma ma
媽媽

man
lan yen
男人

moon
yue liang
月亮

magic
mo shu
魔術

Nn

nest
chueh dow
雀窠

nose
be
鼻

numbers
su szu
数字

one
yat
一

two
ye
二

three
san
三

four
say
四

five
wu
五

1 2 3 4 5

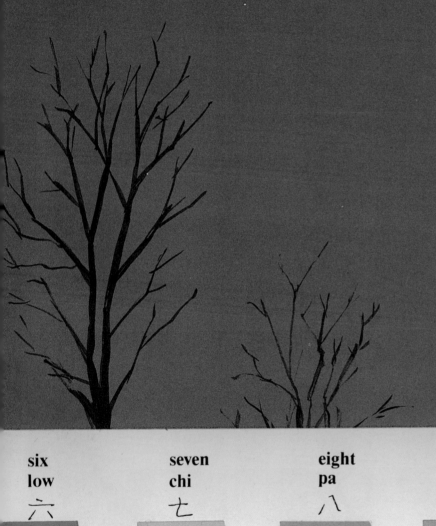

night
yeh man

夜晚

six low	seven chi	eight pa	nine chiu	ten dns
六	七	八	九	十
6	7	8	9	10

orange
chang

橙

owl
mao tou ying

貓頭鷹

oil can
yu hu

油壺

Pp

peach
tu
桃

potato
shu chī
薯仔

peach
tu
桃

pencil
yuan pu
鉛筆

piano
gong come
金岡琴

Qq

queen
wong how
皇后

quilt
men tai
棉胎

Rr

ring
guy ste
戒指

river
ho
河

rainbow
tsai hung
彩虹

rose
mai kuei
玫瑰

Ss

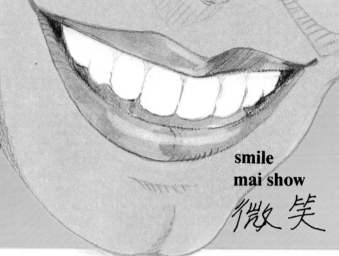

smile
mai show
微笑

shapes
ying chuan
型狀

circle
yuan
圓

square
say fun
四方

triangle
san gor
三角

sphere
kou ying
球型

cube
fun chu ying
方柱型

pyramid
san gor ying
三角型

shoe
hi
鞋

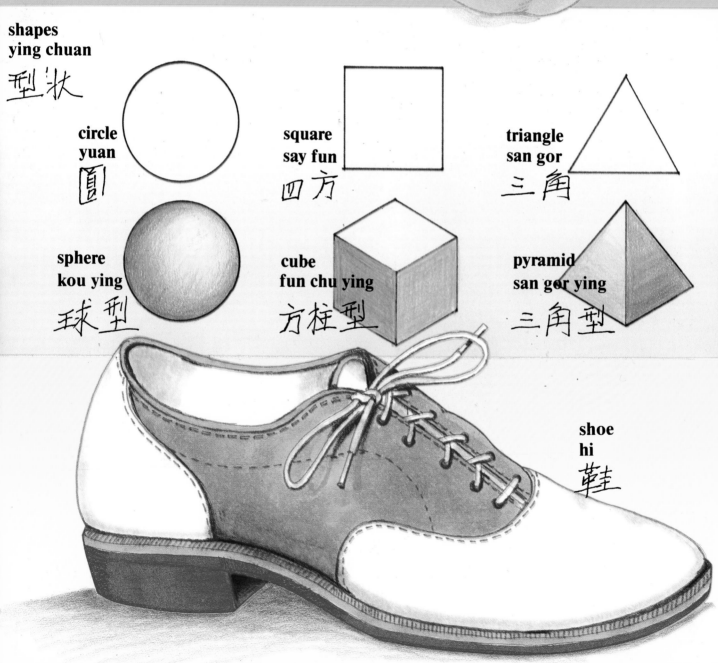

Tt

tree
shǔ
樹

telephone
den wah
電話

turtle
wū gyu
烏龜

Uu

umbrella
yu jě

雨遮

unicorn
do go show

獨角獸

Vv

villain
why yen
壞人

vine
tŭng
藤

vase
fa pen
花瓶

violin
stē-ō ti come
小提琴

village
hung har
鄉下

W w

witch
mao paw
巫婆

water
shsoy
水

window
chan how
窗口

Xx

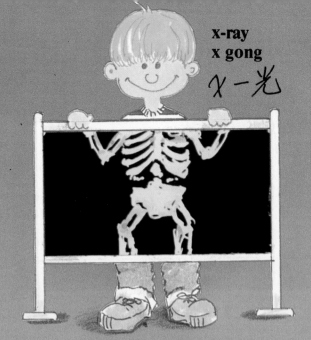

x-ray
x gong
X一光

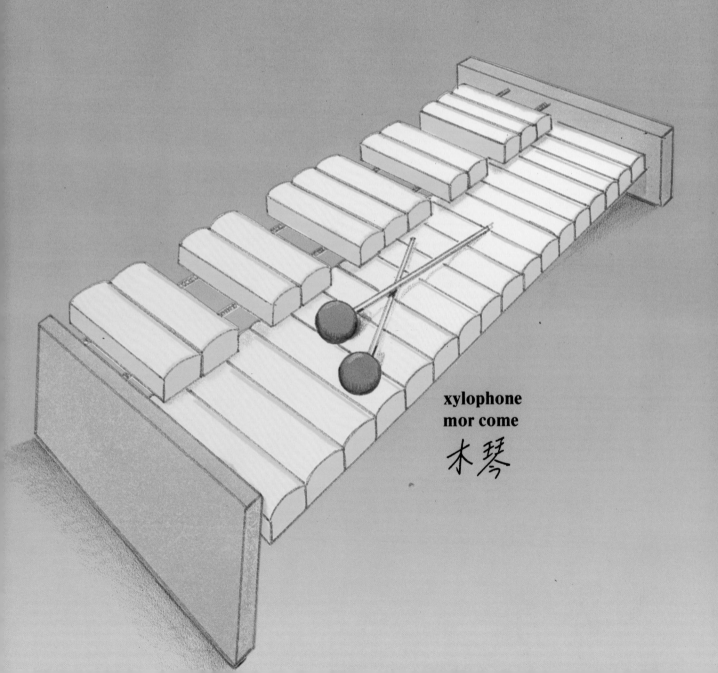

xylophone
mor come
木琴

Yy

yellow
wong see
黄色

yard
yūn
園

yo-yo
yū-yū
搖一搖

Zz

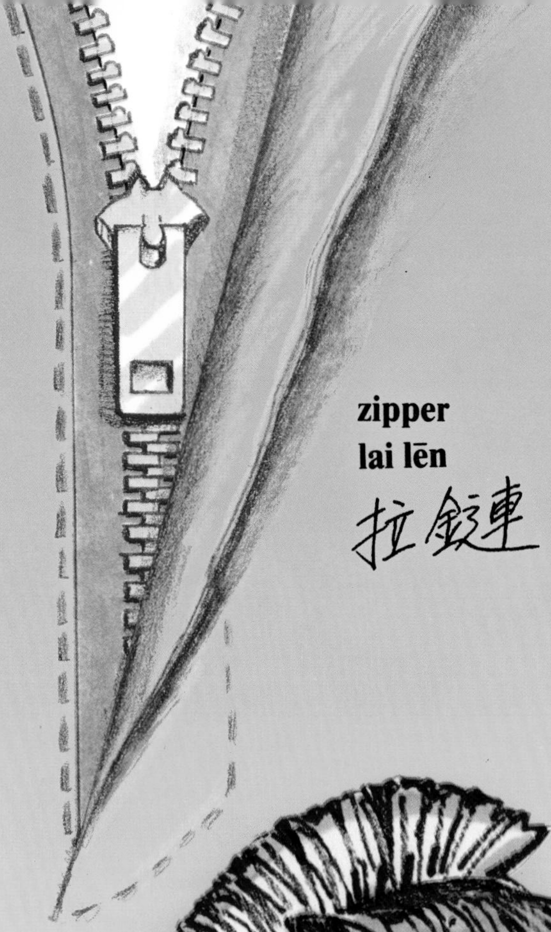

zipper
lai lēn
拉鍊

zebra
ban ma
斑馬

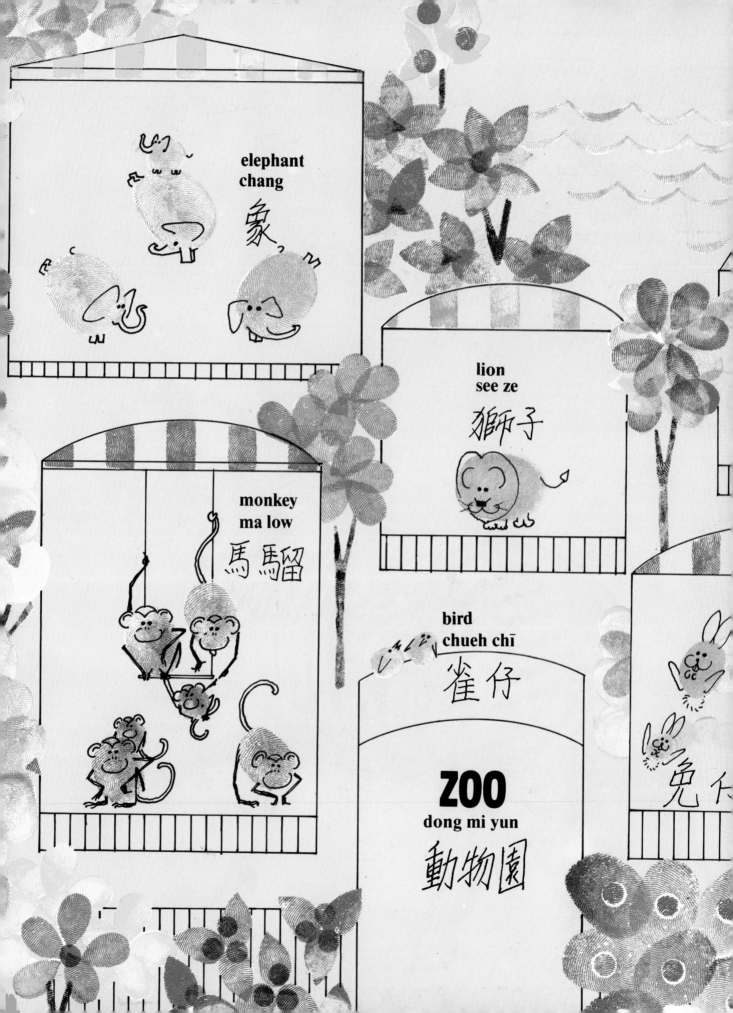